CW00868255

Adventures of the Tooth Fairies

The Wobbler!

By S. de la Perrelle

Illustrations by Corrinne Vaz-Lewis

Copyright © 2012 S. de la Perrelle

Published by de la Perrelle Publishing.

All rights reserved. No part of this publication may be reproduced or transmitted in any form or by any means without the permission of the author.

The right of S. de la Perrelle to be identified as the author of this book has been asserted by her in accordance with the Copyright, Designs and Patents act 1988.

ISBN-13: 978-0-9574819-1-6

ISBN: 0957481918

CONTENTS

ACKNOWLEDGEMENTS

With heartfelt thanks to my husband Alex, my friend and editor
Edwina, Gill and her children Simon and Jamie, to Corrinne and her
children Jasmine, Imogen and Cristiana, my niece Alice, my nephews
Joshua, Matthew and Daniel, and to Lizzy and Sid for all of their
encouragement and support.

1 THE WOBBLER STRIKES!

Crash, bang, clang, clatter! Isabella was rudely shaken from her peaceful slumber.

The roof shuddered and the fireplace tools rattled. Her beautiful white enamel sofa made, of course, from tiny 'milk' teeth, rocked from side to side. As she sat up in bed, she rubbed her eyes, desperately trying to wake from her very deep sleep.

She had been dreaming of far away places, far away from her little cottage in the woods, from her friends and from the life that she so enjoyed in Sussex.

The room rocked again, more furiously this time. Even her white enamel bed swayed backwards and forwards.

Despite being half asleep, she knew exactly what was happening. A little child must be wobbling a loose tooth.

A gently wobbled tooth always sends a message to her – after all she is a tooth fairy – and that message is 'Be on your guard, get ready, this tooth is about to fly free and you must fulfil your duties.' But a tooth wobbled with great force is something quite, quite different. The little child has no idea of the trouble being caused in tooth-fairy land by not letting nature take its course.

Realising that there would be no peace while the child played their game, Isabella jumped out of bed with a mighty flutter.

'Who is waking me up in the middle of the night?' she wondered. She checked the clock and saw that it was only 8 o'clock. Okay, maybe it wasn't the *middle of the night*. But still she had been very tired and had gone to bed early so it certainly *felt* like the middle of the night.

Clearly there was no choice in the matter. She would have to look at her tooth list to see who it was. All the children whose teeth she looked after had their own tooth release schedule, which was safely stored on her computer. This sat over in the corner, away from the pots and pans dancing off the floor, on a highly polished (white enamel, of course!) desk.

The glow from Isabella's log fire made her beautiful desk sparkle as it caught the last hints of light from the dying embers.

As she watched her computer spark into life, another roar came down the chimney, even louder this time.

The rumbles rippled through her tiny cottage, creating even more chaos and more than a twitch of annoyance from Isabella.

A tooth fairy cannot understand why children wobble their teeth. Nature will give up the milk teeth but only when it is good and ready to do so. In a fairy's experience, wobbling causes nothing but trouble.

Isabella is a fair-minded fairy, but, nevertheless, she does find it annoying when children wiggle their loose teeth to try and get the tooth fairy to come early. 'A tooth given in a hurry will always bring worry,' she said to herself.

Often it means that she will get the tooth before it is ready.

All fairy furniture is made from children's white enamel teeth. Chairs, tables, beds, desks – everything.

When a child allows a tooth to come out naturally, it sets properly and will keep its shape for years. But an early tooth is a soft tooth. It wears out too easily and makes very poor quality furniture. A seat will mould into the shape of the sitter, tables become uneven and desks collapse. Imagine a tea party where the tea and cakes roll off the side of the table as soon as they are put down. Disaster!

So very few fairies will keep wobbled teeth because they are simply no use at all. A wobbled tooth is a trouble tooth. The child gives up a tooth that can't be used and the fairy pays good money for scrap.

Sometimes a wobbler, as the fairies call them, will release a tooth far too early, messing up the whole collection schedule. If too many teeth come out at once, Isabella cannot get to all the children's bedrooms in one night to leave them a shiny coin. Isabella has to either give up or risk a daylight trip. Both options are as bad as each other.

The computer glowed in the dark, waiting for Isabella's instructions. Isabella began to smile. She knew her computer would get her the information she needed in a jiffy and very soon she would have a list of culprits to investigate.

Aha! Three children have loose teeth and they all live within three miles of Isabella.

Luck was finally on her side. Her area covered ten miles in each direction, so they could have easily been twenty miles apart.

Another rumble tore through her living room, and one of her favourite enamel vases smashed to the ground. The flowers sprayed all over the floor.

How she disliked the disruption of a wobbled tooth.

A tooth coming out naturally simply sends a tingle down her back and a message to her head. She knows she has work to do. Work that she loves doing as it brings such pleasure to her and the child.

It's a job that unites the fairy and human worlds.

'Why does a child have to wobble?' she sighed. She could never understand it. 'Why upset nature and not let it run its course?'

The three children with loose teeth are Quentin, Felicity and Deepak.

Quentin lives in a very posh house up the hill in Hove. He has plenty of toys; more toys than most children – in fact more than two or three normal children put together!

In short, Quentin is altogether spoilt. He likes to get his own way and rarely says 'Please' or 'Thank-you'. Isabella tries hard not to show any preference towards her tooth-wards (the children she has in her tooth fairy patch) but he is not one that she has ever warmed to.

Felicity is a mild-mannered girl from Brighton. She studies hard and always does what her mum tells her. But that does not mean she is not a wobbler. Wobblers are the most unlikely of children in Isabella's experience.

Deepak is a charming young boy. He lives with his brothers and sisters in Peacehaven and is always very polite and well behaved. Still, he might be the one Isabella is looking for. Not many children realise that a wobbled tooth sends ripples of trouble down the tooth-fairy wire.

Isabella has no choice but to deal with the situation. She must get dressed and head out of her cosy living room into the cold, bleak night to see who has upset the applecart, as the humans often say.

She dragged on her green silk dress with a blue and yellow trim.

The colours are her favourites, especially the green which matches her emerald eyes so perfectly. Her dress clips at the top and bottom of her wings, which shimmer in the light of the dying fire.

She leaves her cottage in a hurry. In such a hurry, in fact, that she forgets to turn her computer off. She flutters up into the sky, away from the trees below.

Leaving the woods behind and entering the city, she starts to smell the human world all around her. Traffic fumes, rubbish bins and the wet tarmac of the road below. She is high above the patchwork of red and grey rooftops, their chimney pots saluting her as she passes by.

She decides to visit the children in the order they appear on her list. That means she will visit Quentin first.

Into Hove she goes, where the winds from the sea sweep up the hill, gathering in strength as they go. She has to flutter harder and harder in order to stay on course for Quentin's house.

Using her fairy magic, she enters his room. He has a big bedroom with lots of teddies and even more cars and plastic toys from the latest craze. Today, he loves Doctor Who and Thunderbirds, but that is bound to change in a week or two.

Isabella sees that he is fast asleep with no loose teeth anywhere to be seen. 'Well I never!' she declares. 'How wrong can a magic fairy be? You cannot judge a book by its cover.'

No time to be wasted – it was Felicity's turn next, the least likely of the three children to be disturbing a nice tooth fairy's sleep.

Felicity was lying in her new Fairy Princess bed, a present for her seventh birthday.

Seven years old and very proud of the number and even more proud of her regal place to rest.

She twitched a little and snuffled a little as she rubbed her small nose with her right thumb. Isabella was captivated by her contentment and was even becoming a little jealous as she watched her sleep.

Something, however, did not seem quite right, but Isabella could not put her fairy finger on what was wrong.

She fluttered around Felicity's room, admiring her tidy shelves, the neat boxes of toys and large book collection. Well, for a seven-year-old, it was very large indeed!

Felicity was just the sort of seven-year-old that Isabella enjoyed working for. Over the years, she would keep a watchful eye over all the children in her patch as their tiny teeth developed. Every child was different. Some would have too many teeth in their tiny mouths which crowded each other out. Some had small teeth and others had big teeth.

Not that Isabella was big herself, she was barely the size of Felicity's thumbnail, but she was a good size for a fairy and that was what counted.

Oddly, Felicity's snuffling and the twitching seemed all too regular and somehow conscious rather than unconscious.

Like all fairies, Isabella can see very clearly in the dark. Although she did not need lights, she knew what the night light glowing in Felicity's room was. It was still on even though she was asleep. Isabella thought it was odd that her mum or dad had not switched it off by now as Felicity was soundly sleeping.

Isabella knew that the light was a great invention for the human species but it was completely useless to a fairy – humans would call this a white elephant.

As Isabella contemplated where the term 'white elephant' came from, and made a note to ask her cousins in Asia if there really *were* white elephants, she remembered that she was there for a reason.

Isabella needed to eliminate Felicity as a suspect in the 'wobbler' investigation.

Could it be Felicity?

2 THE TRAP IS SET

On the surface, everything appeared to be absolutely normal in Felicity's bedroom. But something niggled away at Isabella as she danced in the air around the boxes and shelves.

As she looked away from the sleeping child, she experienced a cold shudder through her wings – the feeling she always got when a child was looking at her.

If a human sets an eye on a fairy, it breaks one of the most sacred fairy laws – 'Never be seen by a human being.' This rule was never questioned and the consequences were never spoken about. It was the natural law that divided the two worlds, fairy and human. If the worlds cross, then the unthinkable will happen. Isabella had no idea what the unthinkable was, as she was not able to think of it, but she knew that she must obey this law for the two worlds to live in harmony.

Another shudder came, colder and longer than before. But Felicity was sound asleep. Isabella could not understand what was happening.

Felicity was a pleasant girl. She had been at school for a couple of years and was doing well at her reading and arithmetic. She particularly liked to read and got absorbed by the fantasies in her extensive book collection.

Fairies and goblins fascinated her. They appealed to her vast imagination and she would lie awake at night wondering whether they really existed or were just 'fairy tales'. When she spoke about this to her mum and dad, they got short tempered. They believed she lived in a fantasy world.

'Don't be so silly, Felicity,' they would say. 'There is no such thing as a fairy or a goblin, can't you tell the difference between reality and fantasy?'

'What do they teach you in that school of yours?'

'Don't you have any homework to be getting on with?'

'I hope your friends are not filling your head with this rubbish!'

Felicity would look at her parents in despair. 'Why don't they believe in fairies and goblins?' There are so many books about them and they seem so very real. 'How could we imagine such things, if they really do not exist? How would that be possible?'

'We know that there are tooth fairies, we know that we get a shiny coin when we lose our teeth,' Felicity would think, 'so how do they think that arrives if they are not real?' It made no sense to Felicity and she would ponder and wonder on the contradiction for hours.

Her parents would tell her the tooth fairy was a game and not real. Something to make losing her teeth more bearable and to have some fun along the way. 'Who was playing this game?' Felicity would wonder. She goes to sleep with a tooth under her pillow and in the morning she would have a shiny coin instead. 'What sort of game was that?'

There was only one thing for it. She would prove that fairies really do exist and show her parents that there was more to life than plain old facts. Sometimes we must believe in our dreams. However, *they* will not believe her without proof, so she would present them with a real live fairy and then they would have to believe!

Isabella noticed a book on the shelf called 'Fairies and Goblins of Furtherland'. 'It's so fascinating,' she thought, 'the humans do not believe in fairies and yet they write about us all the time.' She decided that she would never understand the human race, and a cheeky smile spread across her face.

Isabella fluttered closer to the shelf to take a quick look at the book. She wondered what the humans thought her world was really like.

Isabella was a good and dedicated fairy. But she was also an easily distracted fairy. This was something that her granny had always told her would get her into trouble some day. Isabella was certain that being inquisitive was a gift and not a curse, so it would never get her into trouble. But her granny was rarely wrong about these things and that played heavily on her mind sometimes.

The 'Fairies and Goblins of Furtherland' book was enormous, especially when compared to a little sprite of Isabella's size. Luckily, a fairy can lift human-sized objects using one of their many fairy gifts. All Isabella had to do was to concentrate hard on the book to lift and move it. In exactly the same way, she can carry a coin or get a tooth home.

She was totally pre-occupied now. Isabella started to focus on the book. She was concentrating hard – imagining the book moving off the shelf and onto the chest of drawers below. As she concentrated, the book moved, nudging out of position and floating downwards and landing just where Isabella wanted it. The book opened at the first page, where there was a drawing of what a fairy looks like to a human.

She (it always was a 'she', which amused Isabella as she has many male friends who were definitely fairies) had beautiful blue eyes, wore a silk dress and had shiny, delicate, silver wings and a smile that would melt the heart of a goblin.

In reality, the fairy did not look a bit like Isabella. Fairies are not humanlike, they come from another world. A different world. A special world. Maybe that is why humans say that fairies do not exist. A real one certainly does not look a bit like the picture in the book.

Isabella's thoughts strayed to the boy fairies and how upset they got when they heard that humans think all fairies are girls. After all, they bring their coins for teeth too.

The book was fascinating. Isabella started to read the story. By this time, she was totally distracted. Human words are very different from hers, but she knew enough to understand the tale. She was completely engrossed.

A chill, stronger and longer this time, went all the way through her wings and down her back.

The chill should have been a warning to Isabella to take notice and take care, but the world of fantasy in the exciting book was all she was aware of.

Her wobbler investigation was forgotten and heeding the warnings of the growing chills was quite beyond her now. All she cared about was the unravelling story in 'Fairies and Goblins of Furtherland'.

Felicity had set her trap.

3 BEWARE ISABELLA!

The capture of a fairy would be the talk of the school. Felicity would be the most popular girl around.

On top of this, and perhaps even more importantly, she would get the approval of her parents. They didn't believe her and she was fed up with it. Just for once, Felicity wished her parents would take her more seriously. When she showed them the fairy, they would have to admit that she was right all along. What a great feeling that would be, one she would cherish for a very long time indeed.

Felicity had used iron to set her trap. Yes, iron! A simple metal you could find anywhere. In nails in the tool shed or the garden gate latch, for example. How a little girl of seven years old could ever have discovered that iron has powers over fairies is a tale in itself. Let's just say that her grandmother used to tell her stories when she was younger – tales of fairies and their powers. All of these stories seemed to agree that the only thing that humans have on this earth to make a fairy powerless is iron. It can make a fairy grow very weak, very quickly. So weak that they couldn't even conjure up their basic magic. Once trapped, they would be helpless prisoners for all time. However, take that iron away, move it just a couple of human hand lengths away and the fairy is set free – things return to normal.

Felicity had been developing her plan for a few weeks now. As her teeth got looser and looser, she knew that a fairy visit would only be days away. She would lure the fairy with a fairy book and then creep up behind it to make her 'catch'. The key to the plan's success was her iron box. She was going to slam it down, trapping the fairy underneath. It would be powerless.

A prisoner forever. A pet beyond any pet imaginable. Her own fairy to 'show and tell' *and* get her parents approval, all in one fell swoop.

Isabella was deep in concentration. It is hard for a fairy to read human words, and she was focusing all her energy on the fairytale.

Felicity opened one of her eyes. She had been lying in wait for nearly half an hour.

She was carefully keeping her cover. She did not want to give the tiniest hint to her little visitor that she was really awake.

Felicity had been pulling her tooth to and fro for over an hour, trying to release it from her gum so that she could put it under her pillow. She knew full well that if she was successful, the tooth fairy would have to come. What had taken Felicity by complete surprise was the arrival of the fairy when her tooth was loose, but still in her mouth.

Felicity had to think quickly when she saw Isabella flutter into her room. She kept her cool and realised that this was her perfect opportunity. All the pieces of her plan were in place and she knew what she had to do. She had practised it over and over again, night after night, instead of going to sleep, as she had promised her mum she would do.

As soon as her door was shut at night, she would creep out of bed and pull the iron box out from beside the bookshelf. She would then tiptoe around to the front of the drawers and slam the box down on the same spot. The spot she had chosen was just below the fairy book on the shelf. Exactly where she thought the fairy would be perched. Every night, she imagined her prize inside the tiny iron prison.

The sliding glass top of the box made the cage complete. Inside the fairy would be limp and helpless. The capture would change Felicity's life forever.

No thought was given to the poor fairy's life. No thought was given to all the other children relying on Isabella to place coins in return for their teeth. No thought was given to Isabella's friends and family who would miss her deeply and pine for her every day.

Isabella was quite chilly now, a feeling she was not used to. She never feels the cold the way humans do. Fairies are always at a good temperature. They don't need less clothing in the summer or extra layers in the winter. It's just not the same for fairies. They are never too hot or too cold. They are always just right.

Cold is a warning for a fairy, something to take notice of. It is *not* a signal for a cardigan or a coat. But Isabella was NOT taking any notice of the warning. Instead she was using her fairy powers to thumb through the pages. The story's suspense was mounting and she was lost in her imagination.

Felicity slowly and carefully pulled back her bedclothes as she eyed her prize with glee.

The box was ready and waiting, just half a metre away. She crept on tiptoes to the box and grabbed it with care. The box was heavy because it was made of iron. The weight was a surprise to Felicity, even though she had practised this manoeuvre many times before.

She turned to her prey. With the iron box in her hand, she moved towards the book where Isabella was fluttering up and down above the pages in utter excitement. The box was half a metre away and Isabella was overcome with the equal sensations of cold and fear. Fear was not an emotion that she was used to, anymore than she was used to feeling cold. Something was wrong. The cold was extreme, the fear was paralysing.

Isabella shuddered and fluttered as she became aware of her surroundings once more.

The book was becoming blurred and she was finding it hard to concentrate on reading the story.

Her legs started to wobble, which was most odd as she was fluttering and not resting on them at all. Her arms felt like jelly. Her body was sagging so much that she was hunching over the pages, barely able to hover above the letters. She was extremely confused. Nothing like this had ever happened to her before.

Felicity tiptoed closer to Isabella. Her grin widened and her eyes were nearly popping out of her head. For a moment, Felicity wondered if this was all just a dream. The creature was so tiny, so fragile, so perfect in every way.

Do fairies really exist? Was she really looking at one right now?

4 THE PLAN SUCCEEDS

Isabella started to fall through the air. Her wings were no longer working properly and she was dropping towards the page. She was swaying to and fro like a reed in the wind. Then she started to spin like a plane in trouble, nose-diving towards the ground. Her legs stiffened as she came closer to impact.

Isabella was heading straight for the chest of drawers. It was going to be a hard landing. The book no longer held any attraction for her. The cold and dizziness had taken over and she was engulfed by confusion and a real sense of danger.

Her wings folded inwards and would not open up for flight. She floated down and down, round and round. As she span, she saw a blurred figure. It looked just like Felicity, who had been fast asleep only two minutes ago. What was going on? She saw the bed in the distance. It was empty. It must be Felicity standing there and she appeared to be holding some sort of box. 'What is she doing?' Isabella heard herself wondering.

Isabella had lost her fight to fly. She was now just trying to manage a soft landing.

Maybe Felicity had noticed her plight and had rushed to help. Yes that was it, Felicity wanted to help. Of course, children have always loved fairies. It is only when a child grows up, when they have got all of their new teeth, that they stop believing. Humans are all the same. They grow older and they stop believing, something Isabella had never understood.

Anyway, Felicity was young and a believer. She would help her land and then help Isabella overcome whatever was making her feel this way. Once Isabella was on the mend, she would sprinkle fairy dust into Felicity's eyes and the whole thing would seem like a dream to her.

Isabella wondered whether that was why older humans stopped believing. Was it because fairies take away their memories whenever they were seen? Isabella knew that was what every fairy must do to make sure the two worlds never met. This is fairy law and it must always be obeyed.

Isabella felt more at ease. She had a friend there to help. Someone who would know what to do and how to get Isabella back to normal. Felicity would make sure this unfortunate experience was over in a few minutes, Isabella was quite sure of it.

Isabella saw Felicity come closer, her saviour was trying to help her, even before she crash-landed. How thoughtful, how considerate, how kind. Isabella noticed the box. It was a very odd-looking colour. She has never seen a box like it before. It was a bit like silver but not as bright and certainly not as shiny.

Isabella hoped it was not made from the stuff that humans called iron. Her granny had always warned her not to go near it. 'It will sap your spirit and chill your bones. You will stumble and fall and your wings will crumple into a ball,' she'd said. 'The good news for us fairies is that children do not usually have iron. Only adult humans have it and that is why we don't visit them.'

Isabella always thought that was another reason why adults did not believe in them. Fairies will not go near them for fear of getting too close to iron. Isabella began to panic. 'Could that be an iron box?' she wondered.

Felicity rushed forward with her arm swung back behind her. She lifted the box over her head and then quickly lowered it towards the chest of drawers. Yes! She landed on the very spot that she had practised on for the last few weeks. Isabella was covered with her iron tomb. In a second, Felicity slid the glass lid closed and flipped the box over to peer inside. She saw a tiny figure, with its head lowered over its knees and floppy wings hanging from its back. There was no movement from the creature inside the box. The room suddenly felt quite still, as Felicity stood there in triumph.

Isabella was paralysed. She was trapped in the iron box, confused and dismayed. 'How does Felicity think this is helping me?' Isabella thought to herself. 'I am lying here, shivering and alone, inside this box and feeling as weak as any fairy could ever feel. Why isn't she doing something to help?'

The one good thing was that Isabella could see perfectly in the dark, which was just as well or she might have been even more unsettled and confused. She could see the walls of her prison. They were very close and she felt very shut in. She could barely stand up without hitting her head. There was nothing to look at. Just the four walls or, even worse, looking up into the staring face of her captor.

She tried to flutter her wings which she often did when she wanted to lift her spirits. They would not do as she told them; they just hung by her side, limp and listless. They were acting just as Isabella was feeling.

Isabella had never felt this way before. She was usually very content and went about her day with enthusiasm. Very rarely would Isabella's spirits need a little lift and when they did, she would simply flutter her wings and remember what a gift it was to be a fairy and how much she enjoyed her life in her fairy world.

But this! This was so terrible, so awful, so horrible. She was crouching down in the dark, wondering what was happening to her. She did not know why she felt so weak, or why she had no energy.

Above all, she couldn't understand why Felicity wasn't doing anything to help.

5 FELICITY NEARLY GETS CAUGHT

Isabella heard a noise and then muffled voices. She tried hard to listen but her usual fairy gift of perfect hearing didn't seem to be working. She could make out that there were two voices, but that was all.

When Felicity crashed the box down and caught her fairy prize, the heavy iron box had made a loud bang as it hit the drawers. During her numerous practice sessions, Felicity had been very careful. But in the heat of the moment, she had positively slammed the box into position for fear of losing her trophy.

The movement and noise, in such a quiet house, woke her mum just as she was drifting off to sleep. She sat up with a start.

'What was that noise?'

'Do we have burglars in the house?'

'What about poor Felicity?'

'I hope they are not in her room.'

Felicity's mum tried to wake her dad, but he was very tired and could not be stirred.

She tried to wake him again but as she had no success, she decided to investigate by herself. Of course, that was a silly thing to do if she really thought there were burglars in the house, but she did it anyway.

She crept out onto the landing and listened hard for any further noises but all was quiet again. Maybe she had imagined the noise. Maybe she had dreamt it. Maybe it was all in her head. But it had sounded very real. She really was not sure.

She knew she wouldn't be able sleep unless she made sure that Felicity was safe and there was no-one else in the house. She realised that if the noise was in a dream, nobody else would have been disturbed. So she was careful to be quiet and not wake the entire household for no good reason. She tiptoed further across the landing to Felicity's door, which she carefully and quietly opened, before peeping in to check that all was well.

To her horror, she spied Felicity awake, out of bed at 11 o'clock and standing over her chest of drawers.

'Had she had a bad dream?'

'Was Felicity sleepwalking?'

'What was the explanation for this naughty behaviour?'

Felicity's mum stood at the doorway with her mouth wide open, trying to assess the situation.

'What was Felicity doing? Was she even awake?' In case Felicity was sleepwalking, she decided to enter her bedroom very quietly, 'Just like a church mouse,' she thought to herself. Felicity's mum knew that if a person was sleepwalking, you should wake them up gently and slowly. As the door opened, Felicity froze. She knew that this was going to be trouble. Big, big trouble.

As her mum crept into the room, she whispered Felicity's name, trying to remain as still and calm as possible – just in case Felicity did come around from a sleepwalking trance. 'Felicity, Felicity,' she mouthed with just a trace of her voice leaving her nervous lips, as she watched her little girl standing with her back to the bedroom door. Felicity's mum was now very worried. If Felicity was awake, she would have moved or turned around to see who had entered her room. She would have heard her voice and answered her mum.

She had never had to deal with anybody sleepwalking before. She had heard many stories about it and was not sure what was true and what was not. What should she do? 'Oh dear, oh dear,' she thought to herself.

Meanwhile, Felicity was confused. She was standing in her bedroom in the middle of the night, not in bed, certainly not asleep and she should be in enormous trouble. When Felicity is in deep trouble she is not usually whispered to! She is told what's what, not gently persuaded. Everything about the situation was wrong; very wrong. Mum's behaviour was quite out of character. Why was mum being so quiet with her when she should be having a very different reaction, a loud reaction, an explosive reaction?! Slowly, Felicity turned around and faced her mum, eyes wide open with a look of dread spreading across her face.

Felicity's mum looked at her daughter. The nightlight in Felicity's room was just bright enough for her to assess the situation. It appeared that her young child was indeed awake. However, some say that a sleepwalker can have their eyes wide open and appear awake even though they are in a deep sleep. 'Be careful,' she thought, 'make absolutely sure Felicity is awake before acting.' She whispered 'Felicity, are you awake?'

Felicity looked at her mum in disbelief.

'Had she gone potty?'

'Couldn't she see her standing there in the middle of her bedroom?'

'What was her mum thinking, asking her such a question?'

Felicity was not aware of anyone or anything that can sleep standing upright. Why on earth was her mum asking her whether she was awake?

She thought about her possible answers. She could answer 'No, I'm asleep,' but who in the world would believe that answer? Maybe her mum would as she had actually asked the question. Maybe her mum would say 'that's okay then' and she would go back to her bed and all would be forgotten. Felicity tried to imagine a situation whereby her mum would happily leave her room, go back to her bed and wake up tomorrow morning and not mention the incident, either then or ever again. Not in a month of Sundays, as the expression goes. No way.

So there was only one possible answer in Felicity's mind and that was the truth 'Yes, I'm awake.' It seemed obvious that she *was* awake. In which case, why was her mum asking her? But if it was *that* obvious, surely her mum would be rather angrier than she seemed?

Felicity stood, like a statue, frozen to the spot, staring at her mum, trying to understand what on earth was going on and why her mum was behaving so very oddly.

Felicity's mum stood very still, careful not to alarm Felicity, and growing more alarmed about why she didn't answer. She considered getting dad to give her some advice. Maybe he had experience of sleepwalkers and the best way to wake them gently and coax them back to bed.

However, she decided there was no point calling him. He hadn't heard her when she was right next to him, so how would he hear her when she was in another room? Of course, she could go back and get him but that might disturb and frighten Felicity. The best thing was to continue alone and be very careful, very careful indeed.

'Felicity, Felicity,' she whispered.

She heard a response, a meek little voice breaking the silence, a clear but softly spoken 'Yes mum, I'm awake – are you?'

'What sort of question is that?' thought Felicity's mum. She said: 'I'm standing here in your room, asking if you are awake, if you are alright – what do you mean am I awake?!'

'Well,' started Felicity, 'you are asking me such an odd question. I couldn't think why you would ask me if I was awake unless you were asleep.' As the words left her mouth she realised that her mum must be awake. She was standing there in her room and so she must be awake. Now she was really confused.

'Felicity, what are you doing out of bed at this time of the night?' her mum asked.

Felicity was relieved. It felt very strange. Knowing that her mum was stirring into a frenzy to give her a severe telling off should not have given her a feeling of relief! But, it was much more preferable to the strange behaviour of just a minute or two ago. Much better to have a furious mum than one who was just plain odd!

Felicity pulled herself together. Her mum was still standing there, raising her voice more and more and getting increasingly annoyed by the second.

'Mum, I don't know, I just got out of bed to look at my books because I couldn't sleep,' Felicity lied. She really did not know what to say. No explanation would satisfy her mum, except, perhaps, to tell her the truth. There was no way that Felicity was going to do that. She was in enough trouble as it was. The truth could wait for another day.

'Felicity, for goodness sake, please get back into bed and go to sleep,' her mum said.

The chance to get back into bed without having a major telling off seemed to be her best option, and would probably only be on offer for the next few moments. So Felicity did the smart thing and headed for her bed, pronto. She said 'Goodnight, mum' and crawled in under her quilt, waiting for her mum to make the next move. Her mum sighed and left her bedroom whispering 'Goodnight, and sleep tight,' as she disappeared across the landing into her own room.

Felicity was in a daze. She had captured her prey and alerted her mum to the wrongdoing, but still somehow managed to get away with it – for now anyway. She did not dare get out of bed again to hide her fairy, but the knowledge that the little sprite was there for anybody to find was nagging at her too much to let her get off to sleep immediately. She wriggled and tossed and turned, wondering what she should do. After a while her eyes became heavier and heavier and she drifted further and further towards sleep.

Eventually she dropped off to sleep, worn out from all the excitement. She didn't wake up again until the morning.

6 ALONE AND AFRAID

Isabella listened to the muffled voices but could not make out what was being said. Her mind began to drift into a semi-dream state, nowhere to go, nothing to do.

As her mind wandered, she started to recall the last fairy party she went to. It was last summer, when the sky was bright blue and all the local fairies gathered together to celebrate.

Fairies only get together when the sky is completely clear and blue with the sun shining down on the land. You might often see a clear blue sky with only one small, fluffy patch of pure white cloud in it, not moving despite the gentle breeze, and not changing shape as clouds normally do.

That cloud is in fact a fairy gathering.

To the human eye, even through a telescope, the fairies look like a single cloud against the deep blue sky. It is the only time that humans can detect them during the daylight. The really sad thing is that they do not realise what they have actually seen – a group of tiny beings, giggling, laughing and teasing each other, swapping tales of children who wobble their teeth at all hours of the day and night.

So remember, if you see a white cloud all on its own in the blue sky up above, it may not be a cloud at all. It might be a tooth fairy party.

Isabella remembered that last party well – the friends she shared a joke with, the stories about the close shaves that they have had when they have nearly been caught by the curious children they serve.

Her best friend, Jamie, was there in the group. Jamie was always getting into scrapes, so he always had plenty of stories to entertain the gathered crowd. Isabella loved to listen to his tales, lost among the crowd, but knowing that he was her best friend and had been for many years.

She thought of Jamie and a smile appeared on her grief-stricken face. She imagined his bright blue eyes and his cheeky grin. She could almost hear him recounting his latest adventures as a tooth fairy in this changing world. A world where the children are getting so much smarter and seem to have more and more tricks to try and catch their tiny little night-time visitors.

Isabella's mind drifted back from her happy thoughts to the reality of her dreadful situation.

She was a prisoner. She could not move. She felt cold all over – a sensation that she had never experienced before. She could not understand how the iron stopped her normal powers from working.

Normally, she would be able to flutter her tiny, translucent wings and lift the box that held her with total ease. She should be able to throw fairy dust into Felicity's eyes to wipe her memory, fly out of the house just as she had flown in, and go back to her cosy home in the woods.

But none of this was possible.

Her powers had gone. She lay in her prison alone and forlorn with no way of escape. Isabella was at the mercy of her captor, who had already left her there for several hours and was clearly never going to let her go.

What would become of her? What would be her fate? Isabella had never heard of a fairy going missing before, never known a fairy not to return home. Why was this happening to her?

As the hours passed, she made herself think happy thoughts again, pushing herself to find more memories of fairy parties, of Jamie and of her furry friends back in the woods. Isabella had many animal friends, such as Barak the badger, Freda the fox and Reuben the rabbit. These characters, along with Jamie, made her life complete.

Would they miss her? Would they raise the alarm? What could they do? Where would they look?

As the night drifted away and the morning began to fill the room with daylight, Isabella looked up through the glass ceiling of her iron prison. She lay there, totally exposed for everyone to see. Each and every peek from a human will be striking a blow against one of the most sacred fairy laws: 'Never be seen by a human being.'

If a human does spy a fairy, then fairy dust must be used as soon as possible to wipe away the memory, as if it had never happened. Isabella had no idea what to do if lots of people saw her. How would she track them all down, even if she were lucky enough to escape from her prison?

The longer a human has the memory, the more dust it takes to wipe that memory away. It is even rumoured that if a day or two passes before the fairy takes action, the human will *always* remember. That is why there are fairy books and stories about them. Every now and then, a human sees a fairy and keeps their memory.

Of course, there is also the camera, the dreaded camera. Her granny rued the day the humans invented photography. No amount of dust could rub out a photograph. So the fairies all hope that the lens of a camera cannot see them, the way a telescope cannot see the cluster of fairies that look just like a fluffy white cloud. If a human ever got photographic evidence then the truth would be known. The fairies would forever live in fear of being tracked down and captured in their hundreds.

The fairies' way of life continuing in peace and harmony depends on their existence being a secret from humans.

It was dawning on Isabella just how serious the situation was.

Captivity was terrible for her, but the whole fairy population might also be at risk, just because she was foolish enough to get caught – she was so silly and so careless.

She had to prevent a disaster for herself and her friends.

7 JAMIE TO THE RESCUE

Isabella started to hear noises around her. There was a humming sound as the sun began to rise. 'Perhaps it was caused by the heating these humans use to keep warm,' she thought. Not long after that started, there were footsteps and loud voices. 'Felicity, get up – it's time to get ready for school.' That was Felicity's mum. Isabella recognised her voice from the night before. The household was getting up and she was still a captive. Her worst fears were being realised.

Felicity yawned and stirred and yawned again. There were more footsteps from outside the room, and then a man's voice. Felicity's dad was echoing her mum's instructions. It was 7 o'clock.

Far away in the woods, Jamie was gathering his thoughts, wondering what his duties were for the day. He logged onto his computer and checked his schedule. Two teeth were due to drop out today, three more whose progress needed checking and then he could relax for the rest of the day. Maybe he would see Isabella and the 'furry bunch' (that's what he and Isabella called their animal friends), for a spot of Fairytine and a good old chat.

'Fairytine' is a fairy's favourite drink, hot and sweet and enjoyed any time of the day. The very thought of it made his mouth water.

Jamie was just about to switch off his computer, when he noticed that Isabella was online. She was already logged onto the fairy network and it looks like she had been on there all night.

This was odd, for two reasons.

Firstly, Isabella was well known for being the last to wake up. She was never the first one online. In fact, she was almost certainly the last one to log on to the network each day.

Secondly, she had been logged on for hours. But she rarely left her machine online. It was too risky with all those goblins loading viruses onto the fairy network whenever they got the chance.

'Odder and odder,' he thought, 'what is going on?'

Jamie sent an instant message to Isabella's computer, 'What's up?' He had never been one for long or meaningful messages. When it comes to using the computer, he was happy for the other person to do the typing. Of course, face to face was a very different matter. Then he would chat and joke for hours.

Isabella was always quick to type a note back to anybody that sent her a message. She loved to play on the computer and send messages to her friends, making her quite the opposite of Jamie. Just as it was when it came to face to face conversations, she would sit back and let Jamie chatter away, enjoying listening for hours without hardly saying a word.

Jamie waited for five minutes – the longest it has ever taken Isabella to reply. He looked at the empty screen in disbelief. No response. Nothing. Not even 'Hello.'

Now one thing was certain. If Isabella had night visits to make, she would have turned off her computer before leaving. The situation was highly unusual. Maybe she had a problem, but what would take so many hours to fix?

She should have been home hours ago. Whatever was going on? But then Jamie had a thought. 'Maybe she left in a hurry and then came home very tired and forgot to turn the computer off. I expect she is now sleeping off the night's adventures.'

Jamie smiled to himself. He had an explanation and he had his day to be getting on with. He should not be allowing distractions to interfere with his schedule. Jamie was a fairy who could easily be distracted. Isabella always said that about him when they were teasing each other.

He could be sidetracked at the drop of a hat. He loved anything unusual, anything to escape from his normal routine. Isabella would point out, on an all too regular basis in Jamie's view, that it is the routine that pays the bills and the routine is the reason they exist. They deliver coins in exchange for kids' teeth. That is why they are called tooth fairies!

Jamie picked up his bag and started to make a flutter for the door before taking one last look at the computer screen. 'Oh, now I'm doing the same as Isabella,' he thought, 'leaving the house without turning off the computer!' He went back to shut down his computer before going on his way. Still no response from Isabella. 'I know…,' Jamie thought, 'I will send her a buzz message, wake her up, get a reply. It's about time she got up no matter what may have happened last night.' Jamie sent the message. It would make a loud buzzing noise that would demand that she got up and talked to him.

But, in Isabella's cottage, the buzzing rang around her empty living room, with nobody there to hear. Isabella was far away in her iron cage, completely unaware of the goings on back in the woods that she called home.

Nothing.

Jamie looked aghast at his screen. Nothing, even after that great big noise, nothing!

What was going on and why was Isabella sleeping so soundly today?

Jamie decided that he must know what was going on, or he would be distracted for the rest of the day. In Jamie's experience, distractions make for mistakes, and mistakes get him into trouble, which he can always do without.

Isabella only lived a couple of miles away, down the woods on the left – only ten minutes away when in full flight. Jamie decided that it was not too much of a detour and it was well worth it to solve the mystery.

Off to Isabella's then – there was no choice in the matter. It was only half past six after all, so he did have time.

He switched off his computer and left the house with an added sense of urgency. He was already behind schedule and now he had to call on Isabella. He headed into the woods at full flutter and made his way to her cottage.

As he approached, he saw that the door was shut and everything appeared perfectly quiet and normal, at least from the outside. 'Great,' he thought, 'all appears to be in order. Surely, there's no reason for me to imagine that something awful has happened to Isabella. I will find out that I have been wasting my time, and probably Isabella's as well.' He landed by the front door with a bit of a thud (as he was a little distracted) and knocked on the door.

Knock, knock. He rapped his knuckles against her beautiful wooden door, making a booming noise outside and probably inside too. Silence. He waited patiently. Nothing happened. Nobody came to the door, no welcome in for a quick cup of Fairytine and a chat.

He weighed up the situation again, stroking his chin as he thought, 'Computer on, buzzing ignored, knocking ignored.' Jamie was puzzled. As with all fairies, Isabella has very good hearing. She hears the raindrops falling from the sky onto the leaves outside her door. She even hears Jamie flutter to her doorstep and will often answer the door before he has even had time to knock. And yet today, all of his noisy calls have been unanswered. 'She must be out,' he concluded, 'but where?'

'If Isabella is out,' thought Jamie, 'then there is nothing more that

I can do now to unravel this mystery!' But as he turned to leave her cottage, to get on with his day's duties, he found that he was still feeling uneasy.

Jamie thought long and hard about the situation and decided that he was still not satisfied with things. He had to know where Isabella was and what she was up to. He was sure there was a good explanation. He was certain that his imagination had gone too wild, too crazy, but then again, he was not certain enough just to walk away.

He now had to know for sure.

He tried the front door but it was locked. 'She must be out, but why was her computer on?'

Where was the spare key to the door? Unlike human houses, which a fairy can just enter by magic, a fairy needs a key to get into another fairy's house.

The key was normally hidden under a rock in the garden. Only a few friends knew about this, but luckily Jamie was one of them. 'Which rock was it under, though?' It had been a very long time since Jamie had needed to get inside her cottage when she was not there. He thought hard to try and remember the exact location of the hidden key, but this was proving too difficult a puzzle for him to solve so early in the morning.

'Now where was that key?' he thought. Jamie's thoughts then drifted onto the possibility that Isabella might actually be ill. She might be lying inside the cottage in desperate need of some attention. If that were the case, then he would get her a hot drink and some medicine to make her well again. He then realised that he was pacing about outside Isabella's house, making a noise which would only make her more anxious if she was unwell inside.

Jamie felt an even stronger sense of determination. He had to get inside the cottage.

Then Jamie remembered that Isabella loved rhymes and that she had taught him one to find the key. It all came back to him as he made himself concentrate…

My key is hidden under the big oak tree

In the garden, by the branch on the right

Pull up the stone with all of your might

Please come inside, day or night.

There, above Jamie's head, was Isabella's huge oak tree. It was her pride and joy and the keeper of the secret key.

Jamie reached under the rock at the bottom of the tree and took the bright key from its hiding place.

He unlocked the door and went inside with a big smile on his face, ready to cheer up his best friend in her hour of need.

His face dropped and complete puzzlement took the place of his smile. There was nobody inside but there were signs of trouble. Pots and pans were off their hooks and the bedclothes were untidily strewn over the beautiful enamel tooth bed. The computer sat there with Jamie's messages, delivered but not read. There were no signs of life but there were clear signs that something had happened. Something probably connected to the disappearance of his favourite fairy, Isabella.

He studied the computer screen more carefully. He could see the list of likely tooth wobblers and he quickly pieced together the puzzle. 'It's obvious,' he thought, 'she must have been woken by a wobbler.' She would have gone out on a hunt to put a stop to the disruption. Three names had been on her computer screen since 8 o'clock last night, more than ten hours ago, and she had still not returned. She should have been back by midnight. Two o'clock in the morning at the very latest.

Jamie realised that he really did have a mystery on his hands, something really was wrong. He knew that he had to find Isabella and fast. For once, this was not his wild imagination taking over – he seemed to have been right all along.

There was something very wrong and he had to find out what it was.

8 TIME IS RUNNING OUT

The sun was really beginning to rise now. Jamie knew that if Isabella was in trouble in broad daylight then it was deep trouble indeed. Daytime is when humans can see very clearly, so that is when fairies are most at risk of being seen.

Jamie made a note of the three names and addresses from the computer. He would go and see if they held the answer to the mystery of Isabella's disappearance.

He closed and locked the door behind him, replaced the key in its hiding place and headed to Quentin's house, the first on the list.

As Jamie approached Quentin's house, he could see the reason why he was number one on Isabella's list. Quentin lived in a big home, jam packed with all sorts of wonderful toys and books, perhaps too many for one child.

In a fairy's experience, children who are a little spoilt often live in this sort of house. This can make them a bit naughty and inclined to get up to mischief. Jamie and Isabella have never really understood why such children might be the naughty ones but they just knew it to be true. He quickly entered Quentin's bedroom and surveyed the scene inside, trying to discover if Isabella had been there recently.

Quentin was still getting dressed for school before going downstairs to eat his breakfast. He had just come back from the bathroom with clean teeth and a nicely washed face. 'Oh good, he really did do a nice job on his teeth – he's a good boy for sure,' thought Jamie. Now, was there any sign that a fairy had been around the bedroom? Or for that matter was there still one there?

There were faint traces of Isabella – tiny sprinkles of fairy dust on the carpet, spilt, no doubt, from her pockets (and only visible to other fairies). The room looked generally clean, so the fairy dust must have been dropped recently. Jamie knew that Isabella had no record of being at Quentin's house in the previous week, so she must have been there last night. Isabella might still be in the bedroom. Maybe she was sick or had fallen asleep while reading a book. She gets so easily distracted by books!

'Isabella, Isabella!' he whispered. He knew he had to keep his voice quiet so only a fairy could hear. He didn't want to be discovered by Quentin or any member of his family. A dog barked loudly from downstairs. He grinned to himself. Dogs can always hear a fairy's call. A voice shouted at the dog, telling it to behave itself. The rumblings of discontent about the noisy disruption to the family's morning continued from downstairs while Jamie continued his hunt for Isabella.

It was 7 o'clock and most human households were well into their morning routine of getting ready for work or school. He had to act fast to find Isabella, in case the humans found her first.

Jamie called for Isabella again and this time he added a shrill whistle at the end. This was meant to wake her, in case she had fallen asleep behind a wardrobe or cupboard. The dog barked again, much to the annoyance of the adult downstairs who shouted at it even louder to stop.

Jamie was becoming convinced that Isabella was not in the room. If she had been, she would have heard his calls for sure. He decided he should be very thorough, just in case he had overlooked something. Maybe she could not hear him, or maybe she could hear him but was unable to respond for some reason.

He fluttered around the room, looking under and behind all the furniture. 'It's so odd,' he thought, 'that humans love using wood for their furniture when the enamel in their mouths would be so much nicer. I suppose they just do not make enough for human sized furniture....' Oops, he was getting distracted again and he must concentrate. It was really important that his mind didn't wander.

Around the room once and then again, nothing, Jamie found nothing. No more dust, no more signs of fairy life in the room. He had drawn a big blank.

Jamie decided that Quentin did not have the air of a child who had seen a fairy, and anyway, all of his teeth were present and correct in his mouth. He now felt quite certain that he should not spend any more time here if he was going to be successful in finding his old friend.

It was quarter past seven and he had to move on to the next house on the list – Felicity's.

He fluttered off from Hove to Brighton at a very swift pace. He flew much faster than he normally did and even faster than in his last fairy race, which he had won very comfortably. But now he was in a very different sort of hurry.

Jamie arrived at Felicity's house and wasted no time going through the double glazed window into her bedroom. He hovered by the window, just as a kestrel does when it is stalking its prey. He hung there, seemingly motionless, looking around the room trying to detect any signs of fairy activity from the night before.

Felicity was there in her room, dressed and ready to go downstairs. But Jamie noticed that her attention did not seem to be fully on her day ahead. He could see her gazing towards a grey box lying beside an open book on her chest of drawers.

Felicity looked around the room to check that she was alone and then crept to her door to close it.

Jamie was confused. What was the child doing when she should be going downstairs for her breakfast?

Felicity tiptoed back towards the grey box. Jamie was now sure that Isabella's disappearance was closely linked to this room. His senses told him that she was nearby. He had to find her before it was too late.

Felicity moved closer to the chest of drawers and stared into the box. Her eyes grew wider and wider and her smile grew bigger and bigger. She had a pair of blue woolly tights in her hand, ready to finish dressing, but she did nothing with them. She was lost in thought. Jamie knew that he had to quickly find out exactly what she was looking at in such a strange manner.

Humans can sometimes see a fairy if the light is strong. He had to stay high, near the ceiling, where he knew that humans rarely look. Humans seem to look down a lot – to watch where they are walking, to avoid anything that might trip them up, but they rarely look up. Jamie supposed this is because they never go upwards into the air, the way fairies do.

He hovered high above the drawers and looked down at the box that was fascinating Felicity.

The top was glass – she must be looking at something inside the box. He dropped down 30 centimetres from the ceiling, to try and inspect the box's contents. He wanted to see if it held any clues as to Isabella's whereabouts. Like all fairies, he had very good eyesight, in both the light and the dark, and he could clearly see all the way down to the box below.

Jamie's jaw dropped. He couldn't believe his eyes. There in the box was the last thing he expected to see. It was Isabella, as clear as could be, looking up at the child with tears running down her face. Jamie could not work out why Isabella had not got out of the box in the way that fairies get out of all human-made things. All she had to do was to fly through the glass using her fairy magic and then go home!

Isabella had a pleading look on her face. It was as if she was asking the child to set her free, as if she could not do this for herself. Jamie was flabbergasted. This was beyond his understanding.

Felicity continued to stare at Isabella and was quite oblivious to the noise behind her. The noise was made by her mum coming through the door into her room. She stood in exactly the same spot as she had stood in the night before and waited for Felicity to realise she was there. But clearly that was not going to happen. Felicity's mum opened her mouth and exclaimed in a cross voice that it was nearly half past seven on a school day and that Felicity had to go downstairs and eat her breakfast!

Felicity turned around to face her mum, her blue woolly tights still in her hand and her back firmly to the drawers, hiding the box behind her. Felicity knew, given the events of the night before, that she had to act normally and do everything that was asked of her by her parents. She knew that her mum would not tolerate any more naughtiness so she quickly decided to do exactly as she was told. After all, the box was not going to go anywhere.

Felicity put on her tights and gave her mum a charming smile – one full of confidence and contentment, all at the same time. She walked towards her mum, holding out her hand to be led from her bedroom. She had to avoid any suspicion until she could decide where she would keep her fairy and when she would reveal this magnificent secret to the world. Felicity felt a strong urge to blurt out her wonderful news, but held herself back. She needed to think through her plan before acting.

Jamie was now alone with the box that held Isabella. She had stopped looking up and was hunched over her knees sobbing. Jamie had never seen Isabella sob like this. He could not believe his eyes.

He called out in a shrill voice, the way he had done at Quentin's house, 'Isabella, Isabella!'

Isabella looked up. She could just make out a blurred figure through her tears. Her head juddered as she gasped for breath, and as she did so, even more tears flowed down her face. She had heard something familiar, something heartening, something joyous, but she could not see who was making the sound.

Jamie called again 'Isabella, my dear friend, Isabella.' She wiped the tears away from her eyes. She looked up, trying hard to focus. The metal box had weakened all of her senses. Even seeing a short distance was a struggle. She concentrated harder to try to see who was calling her name.

She could just make out that it was Jamie – high above the box and looking down at her with that smile she loved so much. For a split second the chill of the box left her, she glowed all over and almost felt normal again.

As Jamie started to fly down to investigate further, he began to feel a bit weak, oddly weak. 'It must be all the excitement,' he thought to himself.

Isabella saw him fluttering downwards and screamed at him to stop. 'Don't come any further, stay where you are, please stay where you are, Jamie,' she cried.

Jamie was taken aback. 'Why didn't she want him near her? Why didn't she want to be rescued?' Isabella looked so sad, so much like she wanted help.

He thought about the situation and decided that Isabella must be ill or had lost her powers. That would explain how the child had captured her in the box. Isabella must not be thinking straight. She should know that Jamie was there to help, and that was exactly what he planned to do.

Again, he felt weakened – faint and even a little dizzy. He seemed to lose strength as he moved closer to the box. He instinctively pulled upwards, but it was hard for him to do so. He had less power than normal and his wings were not doing what he wanted.

The further he pulled away from the box, the more his strength returned. Somehow, the box seemed to take away his energy as he got closer to it.

He hovered over Isabella, who was now looking up at him soulfully – trying to smile through her tears. She waved at him and called for him to listen to her. 'Jamie, don't move, stay still and please hear what I have to say.' Jamie did as he was told. He had learnt a long time ago that if Isabella had something serious to say, then he should listen. 'Jamie, the box is made of iron. It has taken my powers away, don't let it take yours too or we will both be in here forever, never to be found or freed.'

Jamie was shocked. 'Oh my goodness,' he thought, 'iron. What was a little girl doing with an iron box? Never mind, that's not the point, I must not get distracted, the point is that Isabella is captive. If I go near her I will suffer the same fate, but if I do not, she may be a prisoner of this naughty little girl forever.'

Isabella pleaded with Jamie to leave her and go and get help. Jamie was torn between staying to attempt a rescue by himself or going to get help. He felt sure that if he left, he would never see Isabella again. Felicity could take her away and hide her anywhere. Jamie would not have a chance of getting his friend back.

Jamie pondered on his problem. He stared at Isabella, feeling both helpless and useless, and not much of a friend at all. He made up his mind – he had to act swiftly and free her. He could not leave her and risk never seeing her again.

As he looked around the room, he tried to work out how he could free Isabella. He tried to think of ways to get close to the box yet not be affected by its obvious powers. He needed something like a stick so he could push the lid off the box without becoming its next victim. He saw a toy box and decided to have a rummage through it to try and find something that might be useful.

He found some glow-sticks that Felicity must have used at the last Halloween or fireworks night. They could be linked together. Jamie decided to make one long rod and try to push the glass lid off the box while remaining at a safe distance. 'Isabella will be free soon,' he thought.

Meanwhile, he could hear footsteps coming back up the stairs, a child's footsteps. He did not have much time. Felicity was on her way back to her room, having finished her breakfast.

He linked a red, green and a blue stick together. Each one was about twenty centimetres long. He had decided that he would need to link at least three together to be at a safe distance from the box.

His heart began to pound as the footsteps got nearer. He had to keep on trying, even at the risk of getting caught. He could not give up now.

Just as Felicity entered the room, Jamie had his red, green and blue glow-sticks firmly joined together. But it was too late. She was back already and he was not even close to beginning his rescue attempt.

Felicity closed the bedroom door behind her and walked towards the bed. Jamie very quietly and gently placed the joined up glow-sticks back in the toy box. He then quickly flew behind the toy box and peeked out to see what was happening.

He wished Felicity would leave her room, just for another minute, to give him a chance to carry out his plan.

Felicity made her bed, as she did every morning before school. She then gathered her schoolbooks and put them into her bag.

All was in order and ready for the day. She just had one more thing to attend to – her prize, her trophy, her fairy!

She moved towards the drawers, eyes widening as she did so, the glow of success colouring her cheeks. She almost skipped up to the iron box and peered inside. There was the fairy, it had not moved, it was hers to keep forever. She was transfixed by the tiny little sprite. Now that her room was so much brighter, she could make out the details of the fairy's wings and hair. She could see how delicate and small all of Isabella's features were – the tiny hands, the smallest of noses, so compact, so perfect, so adorable in every way.

A voice bellowed out from downstairs. Felicity's mum was calling her to come downstairs and get into the car to go to school. Felicity did not know whether to risk taking the fairy with her today. She decided that she had to be very careful about revealing the fairy. She wanted to make the most of the whole affair. She had to be certain that nobody was going to take the limelight from her. She had to be recognised as the only person to have proved that fairies really do exist. Everybody would say how clever she was to have captured one, all on her own.

The voice grew louder and more impatient 'Felicity, come downstairs – NOW!' Felicity panicked – she had to hide the fairy but be careful not to harm it. She could not bear the idea that the fairy might not have enough air and get sick.

She did not want to put the box in a drawer. She knew that she would not like being shut in a box and then shut inside a drawer for the whole day, all alone. So she was not going to do that to somebody else, or was it something else? She was not quite sure.

So the box had to be out but not easily seen. 'Where is a good spot to hide something yet still be a nice place to be left all day?' she wondered.

'The toy box! Put the box on top of the other toys so it does not attract any attention. Nobody clears up the toy box except me, so it is the perfect hiding place for the day.' Felicity beamed.

She picked up the box and moved it towards the toys. Jamie was terrified. He could see what was happening but could not move from his spot, in case he was discovered. If that iron box got too near him, he would lose his strength. All would be lost – they would both be powerless.

As the box came nearer and nearer, he got paler and paler. A chill shuddered through his body – such a terrible feeling, a feeling of doom. He cowered behind the toy box, moving lower towards the floor to try and make sure that he was not detected.

He heard the box being placed on top of the other toys, followed by an extremely frustrated and now quite angry voice from outside of the room. 'Felicity, come here now – if I have to tell you one more time, you know what will happen!!! 1...2....'

Felicity dropped the box and grabbed her school bag, as she hurried out of the bedroom. She knew that getting to '3' meant all kinds of trouble and that is the last thing she wanted. She wanted the opposite. She wanted praise. That was what this was all about.

9 THE DARING ESCAPE

The box had a soft landing on a teddy and then bounced onto a doll. It was not level and as it settled into position, Isabella felt herself sliding towards the side of the box.

Jamie was only half a metre from the iron box now. From his hiding place, he was certain that Felicity had left the room but was careful to make sure before moving too far. He peeped around the side of the toy box and saw a vast empty bedroom. 'Phew,' he thought, 'a bit of good luck at last.'

He flew upwards and looked back down on Isabella once more. She looked forlorn and very tired as she gazed up at him. He smiled at her and said he would free her 'within a matter of moments.' Her look of despair did not change and he could clearly see that she had lost all hope of returning to her wonderful life back in the woods.

He flew to his sticks and immediately began to feel weak again. The box was too close. He concentrated hard, hoping that would help him overcome the cold sensation that was draining his energy. Of course, it didn't.

Jamie grabbed the first red stick and pulled it from the toy box. It was still linked to the others, ready for him to start his rescue mission.

He lifted the long stick and flew towards the metal box, being very careful not to get too close. He approached from the side and moved the stick into position. He lifted it onto the edge of the glass lid and started to push as hard as he could. He had already lost a lot of his strength and it was all he could do to push on the stick. He pressed harder and harder and eventually the glass began to slide. He was overjoyed – he felt that success was only moments away. He smiled, knowing that Isabella would be with him very soon.

Jamie did not hear Felicity's footsteps as she entered the room. He did not hear Felicity move towards him, and he did not notice the look of pure rage on her face as she drew closer and closer.

He pushed with all his might. The lid was now moving. It was open enough for Isabella to squeeze through.

He looked up suddenly and saw Felicity's red face ready to explode. 'Oh no!' Jamie thought, 'not when we are so close!'

Felicity had returned to get the homework that she had forgotten. She had walked into her bedroom and seen the attempted rescue, but then she realised, to her delight, that there was another fairy to capture. She had no doubt that the second fairy had plans of its own – to free the prisoner from its cage and leave her with no fairy captives at all. She moved quickly to try and capture the second fairy.

Felicity swung out her right hand, trying to catch Jamie. He dodged her at the last second and flew up towards the ceiling. Felicity's hand brushed his toes as he accelerated upwards. Felicity tried again to grab her latest victim, but to no avail. She ran and snatched the chair from under her desk, standing on it to reach up higher, as Jamie fluttered up and up above her head.

Meanwhile, Isabella realised that the lid had cracked open enough for her to climb through, but only if she could find the strength to do so. She hauled herself up and put her head out of the gap, breathing fresh air for the first time in hours. She started to heave herself further up by pulling on the side of the iron box. This took away even more of her strength.

Using all of her remaining energy for one last effort, she kicked her legs up and jumped onto the edge of the box, freeing herself from her cage. As she did so, she stumbled backwards and fell into the toy box. She had no energy left to try and prevent her fall. She bounced off different toys as she went, all the time hoping she would come to a halt somewhere soft! She rolled over a doll and then a pair of 'grown-up' play shoes, eventually landing on a jigsaw puzzle deep inside the toy box.

Felicity was still trying to grab at Jamie's feet, as he hovered above her. He had realised that distracting Felicity was a good idea. It had given Isabella a chance to escape.

He watched Felicity with one eye and Isabella with the other. As Isabella tumbled downwards, he took a big handful of fairy dust from his pocket and threw it into Felicity's face. It sparkled as it fell and Felicity looked straight at it, wondering what was happening.

The dust tingled as it landed on her forehead and then in her eyes. Felicity started to look around her and wondered why she was on the chair. She was racking her brains trying to work out what she was doing up there, when her mum came into the room.

Jamie seized his opportunity. He quickly flew up and behind the curtain rail. He was now out of sight. Felicity's mum was standing there in absolute disbelief. 'What was her daughter doing now?' She had been behaving quite peculiarly since last night and now she was standing on a chair in the middle of her bedroom, swiping at the air.

'For goodness sake, Felicity, get off that chair before you do yourself some damage and come here. We need to get you to school now or you will be late.' Felicity was confused – she was on a chair and she no longer knew why. Her mind was muddled, very muddled.

She stepped off the chair and ran to her mum in tears – confused and upset. Her mum hugged her and then became stern again. She forcefully told her to behave herself and come with her to get into the car for school. They left the room.

All was quiet again. Jamie was behind the curtain and Isabella was buried deep inside the toy box.

Jamie called out to Isabella, 'Are you alright? I'm coming to get you now!' Isabella was lying there, unable to move. She had used all her energy freeing herself and had nothing left to help her to climb out from where she had landed. She was a long way down and that iron was still in the way of her freedom.

Jamie flew straight down and headed towards the toy box. He was fearless now – they were so close to success. He wanted Isabella with him and he wanted to get them home. He was not going to let anything get in the way of that plan.

He entered the toy box, staying as far away from the iron box as possible. He could hear Isabella's murmuring as he approached the jigsaw puzzle that she was lying on. He held her hand and asked her how she was.

Isabella felt Jamie's touch and it brought a huge sense of relief. She could finally believe that she would see her house and all of her friends again. She dared to smile. Jamie pulled her by the arm as they started to climb out of the toy box and away from the iron cage. She started to feel her senses return. She felt that she could move more freely, that her wings had become lighter and that the cold had begun to lift from her tiny body.

They headed up towards the light above, clambering over the toys as they went. They looked at each other and smiled. Smiles of relief and pure pleasure, knowing that their ordeal was finally going to be over.

As they got to the top of the box, they both fluttered their wings, letting them spread out either side of their body, ready for flight. They flapped their wings, leaving the toy box behind as they rose up in the air. Gaining strength as they moved further away from the iron.

High up they rose – towards the window and then out, out into the street and away from that 'House of Horrors' as they would later call it when recounting their terrible story to their fairy audience.

Isabella and Jamie flew back to the woods, straight to Isabella's cottage. The computer was still glowing in the corner. Jamie and Isabella looked at it and then at each other. They would never have thought that the computer, of all things, could have helped save Isabella's life. They smiled at each other, out of relief and happiness, so glad to be back in the safety of the cottage in the woods. Isabella walked over to the computer and after reading Jamie's messages, she closed it down. She looked over at him thinking what a smart fairy he was and what an even better friend he had turned out to be.

As for Felicity, from that day on, she lost her fascination with fairies and their stories. She did not know why, but she no longer seemed interested in them. The change in Felicity was a great relief to her parents. They were delighted that she had finally got over her obsession and that life could now continue in a normal way, without all of these fairy tales and silly stories.

The End

ABOUT THE AUTHOR

Siobhan de la Perrelle was born in Sussex, England where she stayed until she moved to Norwich to study for her degree in economics and philosophy.

After graduating, she enjoyed a rich and fulfilling career in technology, starting as a technical specialist and ending up as a global leader with responsibility for people all over the world.

She has varied interests including a passion for travel, nature and the arts. After being lucky enough to travel extensively with her career, she has continued to try and see as much of the world as possible, from Australia, India, South America, Vietnam, Laos and Cambodia to America and Europe.

Siobhan believes that all places in the world have their own special brand of magic embedded in their local culture, variety of wildlife, landscapes and architecture. The wonders of the world never cease to amaze her.

We all know that literature experienced in our formative years not only develops our imaginations but also shapes our attitudes for later life.

With this in mind Siobhan ensures that her books contain a healthy helping of humour, a good pinch of education and plenty of positive underlying messages about mutual respect and good behaviours.

Her children's books are adventures designed to hold the reader's interest and also to give them something to think about along the way.

She hopes you enjoy her work and thanks you for spending the time to get to know her a little better.

www.delaPerrelle.com

17482660R00036

Printed in Great Britain
by Amazon